IMPERFECT

IMPERFECT

poems about mistakes:
an anthology for middle schoolers

Edited by
Tabatha Yeatts

TWEEN

With profound and ardent thanks to Peter Dunlap, Sydney Dunlap, Katherine Rekkas Hewitt, Benjamin Lonske, Catherine Wingfield-Yeatts, Harry W. Yeatts Jr., Ariana Yeatts-Lonske, Dashiell Yeatts-Lonske, and Elena Yeatts-Lonske for their stalwart service. Special thanks also to Michelle Heidenrich Barnes, Margarita Engle, Charles Ghigna, and Keri Collins Lewis for their serendipitous support.

Cover design and interior artwork by Vivien R. Zhu © 2018

Hardback ISBN-13: 978-0-9679158-3-8
Paperback ISBN-13: 978-0-9679158-2-1

History House Publishers
Rockville, MD, USA

mistakesanthology@gmail.com

This book is dedicated to
imperfect people
everywhere

THE STORY BEHIND THE COVER

When we make mistakes, show our imperfections, or wind up feeling broken in some way, we have to patch ourselves back together. The Japanese art of *kintsugi* is the art of creating "precious scars" or "golden repair" by filling cracks in pottery with precious metals such as liquid gold or silver (like the vase on the cover of this book).

Kintsugi is said to have begun hundreds of years ago when a Japanese military commander broke his favorite tea bowl and sent it to be repaired. When the bowl returned, it had been patched together unattractively with metal staples. Seeing the well-loved but sloppily-mended bowl inspired Japanese craftsmen to develop kintsugi as a better, more beautiful way to fix something broken.

The breaks in kintsugi pottery are considered to be part of the object's history, and are displayed with pride. An imperfection isn't the end. It's a chance for a "golden repair"!

TABLE OF CONTENTS

INTRODUCTION

Who makes mistakes?

Do only people who are "faulty" in some way make mistakes? People who don't try hard enough, people who are a little bit "bad"?

That's how I felt when I was young. It made me upset and angry when anybody pointed out my mistakes. Saying "I'm sorry" was hard because it meant I was admitting I had done something wrong...and if I didn't apologize, maybe I hadn't done anything wrong! My logic there was pretty messed up, because whether I had done something wrong didn't depend on whether I said I was sorry. Eventually, I recognized that, and I also realized that every single one of us makes mistakes – no exceptions.

Nick Foles, quarterback of the Philadelphia Eagles, said after their Super Bowl LII win, "Failure is a part of life. It's a part of building character and growing. Without failure, who would you be? I wouldn't be up here if I hadn't fallen thousands of times, made mistakes. We are all human."

Some mistakes are made because we just don't know enough. We don't know that someone is having a bad day and that what we say will make them feel worse. We think no one will see the photo we take or read the private note we write, and it turns out we're wrong. Things don't unfold the way we expect because we don't know the real situation or we assume something that isn't true. We make decisions all day long, with just the information we have on hand.

One time, I made brownies for a family friend who was feeling low and tired, and we discovered later that the reason he was feeling bad was because he couldn't digest wheat flour. (Fortunately for my conscience, he wasn't hungry and other people in his family ate the brownies, so I hadn't made him feel worse.) Even good intentions can lead to mistakes. What's a person to do?

There are a few things we can do. Of course, we're always going to try NOT to make mistakes. We don't want to have to be cleaning up messes – literally AND figuratively.

One thing that helps is to learn from our past blunders. Another is to learn from each other's slipups. As author Brandon Mull said, "Smart people learn from their mistakes. But the real sharp ones learn from the mistakes of others."

Scientists and inventors build on what has already been tried and ruled out. Failures are information, a way that doesn't work. It's valuable to know. But you don't have to be a scientist to want to know what not to do!

In this anthology, you will find poems about all kinds of mistakes. Ones that resulted in a discovery, like *Persistence, or In Praise of Post-It Notes.* Ones where the person didn't know enough (but thought she did), like *Know-It-All.* Ones where the person just had to laugh afterwards, like *Perplexed*, and ones where the person was filled with regret, like *To the boy playing with his army men on the front lawn.*

You'll also find poems about dealing with people whose mistakes hurt us. Do we look for love in our hearts, or peace, or sometimes, do we just have to peel their words away? Every situation is different, so our response won't always be the same.

Author Kellie Elmore said, "Poetry will die when love and pain cease to exist." We're still doing what humans do, making mistakes, feeling love and pain – so poetry is alive and well, thriving here in your hands.

TABATHA YEATTS

SYLLABUS FOR EIGHTH GRADE

Throughout this course,
we'll explore the art of being thirteen
going on fourteen.

We'll practice sitting on a chair
without falling on the floor,
posting in the class group chat
without hurting anyone's feelings,
having a crush on a ninth grader
without losing your dignity.

In our year together,
we'll entertain a range of emotions,
with frustration being a frequent visitor.

We'll experience rejection,
heartbreak,
elation,
humiliation:
some days, all before lunch.

There are tissues on the teacher's desk.

Bathroom humor will be tolerated
on a limited basis.

The teacher will try not to roll her eyes at you
if you try not to roll yours at her.
We'll read what many others have written
about being alive,
and we'll write what we think and feel,
or at least some of it.
Some of it we'll bury on the playground

when nobody's looking.

Evaluations will be gentle,
since nobody has ever mastered
the art of being thirteen
going on fourteen.
Or any other age, really.
We're all just figuring it out as we go along.

Ready? Let's begin.

RUTH HERSEY

ONCE UPON A TIME

Once upon a time,
there was a girl
who never made a mistake.

Which is why
this is
a fairy tale.

APRIL HALPRIN WAYLAND

WHAT GOES WRONG?

Mistakes flower
Every hour.

Ice cream, dropped.
Joke, flopped.

Tire, flatted.
Jump, splatted.

Directions, lost.
Guidance, tossed.

Trousers, muddied.
Quiz, unstudied.

Pencil, broken.
Truth, unspoken.

Team, beaten.
Homework, eaten.

Laundry, pink.
Armor, chink.

TABATHA YEATTS

HAIKU FOR HOW TO SCREW UP MIDDLE SCHOOL

Hit the snooze button
just this once, oh just once more?
You will miss your bus.

Apply mascara
in your locker's reflection?
You'll get a black eye.

Pass notes in science –
learn more than you wanted to
on cause and effect.

Why not give hot lunch
another try after all?
Because: this meatloaf.

Reading the SparkNotes
instead of Johnny Tremain?
Well, that didn't fly.

Why did you sign up
for French horn when you're not French
and can't hold a tune?

When you're pretending
to be like everyone else?
You will lose yourself.

Equilateral
is different from elliptic
and equidistant.

Asking anyone
to keep a deep dark secret?
Doesn't seem to work.

The smell of this gym
answers all questions ever.
Laundry does matter.

Will this never end?
Middle school's not forever.
You can do this thing.

LIZ GARTON SCANLON

MISTAKE

a diamante

Mistake
colossal, grievous
blunder, trip, tumble
assumption, error, chance, risk
venture, strive, try
rare, golden
opportunity

LINDA MITCHELL

MISTAKES-SEKATSIM

Mishaps
Inconceivable,
Slip-ups and
Trip-ups,
Are
Keenly painful
Events that
Sharpen our
Skills,
Eventually resulting in
Knowledge and
Agility, but
They can only be
Seen clearly
In a rear-view
Mirror.

DONNA JT SMITH

Perhaps it is our imperfections
that make us so perfect for one another.

JANE AUSTEN

I'm not perfect,
but I'm perfect for you.

GRACE JONES

A DEFINITION
(excerpt)

YOU ask me, What is love?

It is to see as far, as clear as a falcon,
And stumble over a stone in the path before you.

JAN STRUTHER

MISTAKEN IDENTITY: A POEM FOR TWO VOICES

We thought it would be funny.

To pretend

to be each other

just for one day

just like Fred and George Weasley

or those girls in "The Parent Trap"

or every other set of identical twins

in the history of ever.

We thought it would be funny . . .

Until the moment it worked

Until it worked too well

And SHE got

my first kiss!

KERI COLLINS LEWIS

MISS TAKEN IDENTITIES

Fear not, though doomed to miss no mess,
We're blessed with cleverness
When we can simply take
And shake
Miss Guided's hand in stress!

Miss Spelled, Miss Read, Miss Understood
Could help us if we would
Consider all their flaws
And pause –
Convert Miss Deed to good!

Miss Take arrives with time to spend,
Embrace this dreary friend;
Discovering her worth
With mirth
Will help you learn to bend.

Miss Step leaps in through open door
And whirls you round the floor;
Proclaims aloud to all,
"A fall!"
She's so hard to ignore.

Miss Spoken's words come all unglued
Until you may sound rude;
Slow down, reflect, respect,
Inspect –
She could be Miss Construed.

Your pail may break, your milk might spill,
Your shoes with liquid fill;
Don't let Miss Hap's pure joy
Destroy
Your rolling trip downhill.

Though in your walk you may feel lost,
In mist and wind be tossed;
Defeat Miss Led, just try
To spy
Where Miss Aligned was crossed.

Mislay your misery and woe,
Misplace your misnamed foe;
Let no Miss Givings steer
You clear
Of what you need to know!

DONNA JT SMITH

EXPERIENCE

This morning I looked at the map of the day
And said to myself, "This is the way! This is the way I will go;
Thus shall I range on the roads of achievement,
The way is so clear—it shall all be a joy on the lines marked out."
And then as I went came a place that was strange,—
'Twas a place not down on the map!
And I stumbled and fell and lay in the weeds,
And looked on the day with rue.

I am learning a little—never to be sure—
To be positive only with what is past,
And to peer sometimes at the things to come
As a wanderer treading the night
When the mazy stars neither point nor beckon,
And of all the roads, no road is sure.

I see those men with maps and talk
Who tell how to go and where and why;
I hear with my ears the words of their mouths,
As they finger with ease the marks on the maps;
And only as one looks robust, lonely, and querulous,
As if he had gone to a country far
And made for himself a map,
Do I cry to him, "I would see your map!
I would heed that map you have!"

CARL SANDBURG

APOLOGY

I'm sorry for my oversight,
my flub, my goof, my slip,
my lapse, my glitch, my sin, my gaffe,
my fluff, my muff, my trip,

my botch, my bungle, my faux pas,
my misstep, my miscue,
my blunder and my carelessness,
my blooper, my snafu,

my mess, my impropriety,
the chances that I've blown,
my fumbles, my mismanagement,
the things I should have known

but didn't, cause I went too fast
and could not reach the brakes.
I'm only human, don't you know?
And humans make mistakes.

ROBERT SCHECHTER

Silliness is sweet syrup
that helps us swallow
the bitter pills of life.

RICHELLE E. GOODRICH

THE GRAND AND GLORIOUS SUPER-DUPER ICE CREAM CONE

I thought I'd make an ice cream cone
that almost reached the sky.
I'd be the envy of my friends
with ice cream heaped that high.

I plopped three scoops of chocolate chip,
two salted caramel core.
But why a five-scoop ice cream cone,
if I could add some more?

I scooped on maple walnut
and peppermint surprise,
my grand and glorious ice cream cone
was getting pretty high.

Seven's great but still too small—
so more must go on top.
I piled on some cookie dough,
then peanut butter cup.

Banana berry, candy crunch,
fruity lemonade—
This is the grandest ice cream cone
that I have ever made.

My super-duper ice cream cone—
it almost reached the sky.
I'll be the envy of my friends
with ice cream heaped this high.

I walked outside and strolled about.
My friends cried "look at THAT."
Then my majestic ice cream cone
suddenly went splat.

E.K. TAYLOR

VAMPIRE VS. VENTI

Bec LeCru rose at sundown as normal.
He dressed in black, as usual—formal.
He stopped at the all-night Starbucks for coffee.
He ordered espresso with two shots of toffee.
The barista's mistake: serving decaffeinated.
Bec fell asleep
          with his face
                    on the table;
Dawn found him dead, sadly decoffinated.

HEIDI MORDHORST

A LANDLUBBER'S TALE

Young Pirate Paul couldn't take any more
of the waves and the ocean's perpetual roar—
and the fact that his chores were a bone-crushing bore
did nothing to raise his morale.

He dreamed of the day he'd debark on the shore,
find a house where he'd keep his feet fast on the floor...
but one day while swabbing he tripped on an oar—
now he's bobbing off Guadalcanal.

RENÉE M. LATULIPPE

THIS IS JUST TO SAY

after William Carlos Williams

I have lost
the boomerang
that you brought
from Australia

and which
you were probably
saving
for posterity

Forgive me
it was homesick
and wanted
to return

MICHELLE HEIDENRICH BARNES

MY TROUBLES STARTED EARLY

My troubles started early as I lay fast asleep, my head beneath
a pillow, my blankets in a heap.
A troll turned off my alarm clock; it didn't ding-a-ling.
It had to be a troll, I swear, they do that sort of thing.

I awoke, saw the time, and jumped into the shower
where a python slithered up the drain for something
to devour.
He drooled hungrily at me, and seeing certain doom,
I slammed the bathroom door and sprinted dripping
to my room.

I hustled to the closet and – what do you suppose?
A pesky poltergeist burst in and rumpled all my clothes.
It overturned my bureau, it flipped me in midair.
Somehow I jumped into my jeans and finger-combed
my hair.

Downstairs for a yogurt – my favorite, French vanilla.
Reaching for a banana, I bumped into a gorilla.
The hairy beast scowled back at me – my signal to vacate.
I ran out and left him there! That's why I'm so late!

SUSAN WEAVER

POPCORN

Pip
Pop
Pap
Ping
Pang
Zing
Zang
Fluffy
Puffy
Poofy
Light
White
Popped
Corn

Next
time
though
maybe
we
should
use
a lid.

E.K. TAYLOR

PERPLEXED

I texted her "We're at Big Wok—the one near Central Park"
So why was her text back to me
only question marks?

I looked back at my text to see what my fast fingers sent...
and what it said was crazy—
it wasn't what I'd meant!

It said we were at Bug Works...
what could she have surmised?
Beetles, wasps and bedbugs—and every dish stir fried.

APRIL HALPRIN WAYLAND

As long as the world
is turning and spinning,
we're gonna be dizzy
and we're gonna make mistakes.

MEL BROOKS

THEN LAUGH

(excerpt)

Build for yourself a strong box,
Fashion each part with care;
When it's strong as your hand can make it,
Put all your troubles there;
Hide there all thought of your failures,
And each bitter cup that you quaff;
Lock all your heartaches within it,
Then sit on the lid and laugh.

BERTHA ADAMS BACKUS

TROUBLES IN STORE

Now my troubles are going to have trouble with me!
~Dr. Seuss, *I Had Trouble in Getting to Solla Sollew*

I was not far from home. I was out for a walk,
When I saw a new store, right here on our block,
And a bright yellow sign that filled me with cheer,
"Troubles R Us—Get Your Troubles Right Here!"

Now, troubles are something that I really savor;
Their sumptuous richness! Their delicate flavor!
So I went in and said, "I like troubles a lot:
I'll take a big bag. Fill it up to the top!"

"Give me some of each kind! I'll try them! I'm willing!
And don't forget those with the caramel filling!
Enrobed in dark chocolate! And milk chocolate too!
With crystallized violets! And buttercream goo!"

"Troubles for breakfast! Troubles for lunch!
Troubles at tea-time and snack-time and brunch!
I'll eat six at a time; I'll be sure not to waste them.
Troubles galore! I can already taste them!"

"Praline and cashew! Rum, raisin, and cherry!
Peanut and almond and walnut raspberry!
Pink marzipan roses! Nougat ribbon ruffles!"
He replied, "We sell troubles. You're thinking of *truffles*,"

"Which *are* quite delightful. Your taste is exquisite!
However, since you bothered to stop in and visit,
Please take some free samples—no charge whatsoever!
We value your business; we applaud your endeavor!"

I couldn't refuse; the things looked delicious.
They even appeared to be slightly nutritious,
so I reached right in and grabbed a big scoop,
Filled it full as I could, and then ate 'em right oop.

Their texture was odd, and I started to worry;
Before I got out of the store I was sorry.
By the time I got home I was sick! Yes indeedy,
I certainly learned not to be so darned greedy.

My hearing was troubled, and so was my blood;
My liver and lights did not work as they should.
My intestines were writhing in horripilations!
All in all, I experienced painful sensations.

Learn from me: you'll more likely avoid any trouble
If you learn to pronounce—and spell—before you gouble.

F. J. BERGMANN

BARBER SHOP

Beneath a barber sign
my sister opened shop.
Winding in a lengthy line
sat children with unruly mops.

She lathered, foamed;
she rinsed and combed;
she trimmed and clipped;
she buzzed and snipped.

For each who nestled in her chair
she gave the latest styles,
and clips and snips of cut-off hair
rose up in mounting piles.

She's waiting for more customers though—
waiting for more hair to grow.
For now her work has somewhat stalled—
since all her dolls are fully bald.

E.K. TAYLOR

DRAGON'S PICNIC

Damsel and dragon rambled about
down by the moat
where the fireweeds sprout.
They spread their blanket
with ham on rye
and for dessert: a birthday pie.

"Blow out the candles,
Bubba, dear."
And Bubba did…
he did, I fear.

For damsel had forgotten
the bulbous snout
from which Bubba breathed
his fire out—and out
it poured, a roar, a hiss
that startled our sweet
picnicking Miss.
She stared in alarm
at her crispy, singed hair –
then dear Bubba binged…

Mmmm. Damsel,
medium rare.

RENÉE M. LATULIPPE

THE WORKS

I ordered a pizza
with everything on it—
it took me by surprise.
For when it arrived
it was heaped so high
it almost reached the skies.

With bed-springs
and shoe strings
and bat wings
and a bicycle build for five.

Hat racks
and mouse traps
and thumb tacks
and a very buzzy beehive.

Parts of a truck
a rubber duck
a hockey puck
a grandma out for a drive.

Pink flamingos
and garden hose
and several crows
who were very much alive.

Next time I order
I'll be much more clear
I'll tell them, I think
whatever they do
to leave off the
kitchen sink.

E.K. TAYLOR

A NOTE FROM THE ARCHITECT

I didn't mean
for my tower to lean —
my work is usually not sloppy.

At least I know
that history will show
my creation will never be copied.

MARY LEE HAHN

TEN FORECASTERS

ten forecasters
all wrong...
rain on the blossoms

KOBAYASHI ISSA

TITANIC REMEMBERS APRIL 16, 1912

My maiden voyage
interrupted by an iceberg
clawing at my hull.

And still my engines
chugged, unsinkable
unsinkable unsinkable.

Alas, my armor could
not hold: I tipped like a top
and dipped ever so slowly

lower
    and lower
        into the icy Atlantic.

Oh, my passengers
and crew, how I failed you!
Not enough lifeboats,

not enough time for rescue.
In the end, what could I do
but sink and hide?

It's true a ship cannot cry,
but every day I mourn
the many lives lost

that bleakest
    blackest
        night.

IRENE LATHAM

THE ALASKA PURCHASE

a double dactyl

In 1867, United States Secretary of State William H. Seward agreed to purchase the Alaska Territory from Russia. His critics called the Alaska purchase "Seward's Folly." Later, once gold was discovered in Alaska and the value of the vast natural resources of the northwestern territory became apparent, Russia's price of less than two cents per acre for the sale appeared to be the bigger mistake. Yakutat Bay was settled by Russians in 1795; Kodiak was the capital of Russian Alaska.

Shivery, quivery,
Kodiak, Yakutat:
Seward paid Russia for
acres of cold.

Buying Alaska? Such
irrationality!
Naysayers protested –
till they struck gold.

CHRISTY MIHALY

There are no mistakes,
only happy accidents.

BOB ROSS

DO ANOTHER TAKE

Don't be *mis*-led!
A *mis*-take is simply a *mis*-step.
Don't have *mis*-givings.
Do another take.

If a potter's bowl *mis*-fires in the kiln,
she does another take.
If a mathematician *mis*-calculates,
she does another take.
If a movie director's shot *mis-takes*,
she does another take.

A *mis*-take is not a failure.
Do another take.

B. J. LEE

I TOLD MY CAT

"Many of life's failures are people who did not realize how close they were to success when they gave up." ~ Thomas Edison

I told my cat what Edison said,
and she agrees that my biggest
mistake would be to give up.

I keep at it—this equation—while
Cat bats my pencils to the floor.
They roll. Only she knows where.

I spent hours last night. More
today. I will get it. I will get it!
Cat gives me an approving nod.

She says, "You will not be a failure!
But, we may run out of no. 2 pencils."

DIANE MAYR

IN THE ARCHIVE

Something that will never cease to delight
& surprise me: how some teenagers seem
not to care for belongings of the dead,
until they do. Poring over browning
papers, full of familiar witness marks
and unfamiliar stains, one looks to me,
"It's math. Is it calculus?" "I think it's
physics. Einstein's. What do you think it means?"
"Don't know German." We come upon scratch-outs.
"Wait, this is Einstein making a mistake!"

PATRICK WILLIAMS

TARZAN AND THE MANGANI MISTAKES BY EDGAR RICE BURROUGHS

In 1912, Edgar Rice Burroughs wrote Tarzan and the Apes, a book about a baby who is adopted by a gorilla. This book became very popular and was made into tv shows, plays, and movies.

Sabor was a name once invented by
Me for tigers in my books. (I had
Invented a language called *Mangani*
Spoken by the Great Apes and Tarzan). Bad
Tigers roamed through Africa and fought with
Tarzan... then I learned there were none of those
There! I changed *sabor* to mean 'lion'. Word-smith
That I was, it was easy. But I chose
An animal the Great Apes already
Called a *numa* in the books. But what would
I do? It occurred to me that maybe
Numa could mean lion and *sabor* could
Be a word to use for a lioness!
Whew. I made and fixed those mistakes, *rak* (yes).

JULEIGH HOWARD-HOBSON

PERSISTENCE, OR IN PRAISE OF POST-IT® NOTES

Those little sticky notes that peel off and then stick again to another surface are the result of a mistake! A scientist who was trying to develop a strong glue ended up inventing a not-so-sticky adhesive that could be reused. For years he talked about his glue as the "solution without a problem" and eventually another scientist developed the idea for what became Post-It® notes. But even that product took years of testing, market studies, and renaming before it became popular. Persistence pays off!

The span of time from
Oops
to
WOW!
holds the story of when and how
something new from mishap came
and turned to gold the straw of shame.

Failure shows the reason why
success waits silently,
standing by,
hiding in plain sight and then
you pause
and look
and try again.

KERI COLLINS LEWIS

MAKE A MISTAKE FOR GOODNESS SAKE!

Make a mistake for goodness sake!
Take a risk in being wrong.
Listen to a different drummer.
Write the words to your own song.

Be wild and woolly whenever you can.
Be foolish and daring and brave.
Be silly and fun. Skip when you run.
And try not to always behave.

Be honest and fair. Act like you don't care.
Be loving and caring and free.
Just be yourself. Take care of your health
And don't listen to people like me.

CHARLES GHIGNA

An arrogant person
considers himself perfect.
This is the chief harm of arrogance.
It interferes with a person's
main task in life –
becoming a better person.

LEO TOLSTOY

REJECTING HARRY POTTER

a double dactyl

Author J.K. Rowling has said that her manuscript for Harry Potter and the Philosopher's Stone (the British title) was rejected by a dozen publishers before it was finally accepted. More than 500 million copies of the Harry Potter books have now been sold worldwide.

Hippogriff, schnippogriff,
Salazar Slytherin –
publishers dissed Rowling's
Sorcerer's Stone.

"Magic won't sell; we need
marketability!"
They'd be much richer, had
they only known.

CHRISTY MIHALY

ANACONDA SURPRISE

Dressed in
a river's disguise,

they coil
and hide,

eyes alert
to movement

of caiman
and capybara.

What do these
jungle giants think,

when they
become prey

for a scientist
wading the
Amazon

with no shoes
on his feet?

IRENE LATHAM

KNOW-IT-ALL

Los Pinos, Cuba, 1960

My great-grandmother's lean yellow dog
doesn't have a collar, leash, soft bed,
or normal name, just Perro: Dog.

He follows my bisabuelita all over her garden,
hunting crickets, chasing lizards, and protecting her
from friendly
cats.

His meals are leftover rice and beans,
no canned food or kibble, and since I'm smart,
I decide to ride a crowded bus all the way
to downtown Havana, where I buy
exactly one can
of expensive
imported
North American
dogfood.

It looks like mush and smells like poo. P.U.
Or Pee-yoo. I'm smart, but I'm not really sure
how to spell the sound
of a foul smell.

Perro gobbles my generous gift, then promptly
throws up, making everything even more

stinky
and sad.

So I guess it's true, what my mother says –
great-grandmothers really do
know a few bits
of wisdom.

Perro is a happy, healthy dog
as long as he's allowed to run free
and eat simple dishes
like boiled rice
with raw crickets
his favorite
treats.

MARGARITA ENGLE

UNAWARE

There once was a boy from Gno
who thought he knew all you could know.
He named countries and states
without one mistake,
but he didn't know what he didn't know.

BONNIE SCHUPP

SOME POSITIVE PERSISTING FOPS

Some positive persisting fops we know,
Who, if once wrong, will needs be always so;
But you with pleasure own your errors past,
And make each day a critique on the last.

ALEXANDER POPE

The difference between school and life?
In school, you're taught a lesson
and then given a test.
In life, you're given a test
that teaches you a lesson.

TOM BODETT

DEAR MS. PARTRIDGE

My thoughts,
journal-jive,
honey-hive,
private beats,
micro-tweets,
are music
not mistakes.
I write in pulses.
You can hear
if you try
but don't pry.
Words are birds.
They find the sky,
flying high.
Don't judge
every smudge,
just read,
words bleed,
take seed,
fill a need.
Hear my song
because my words
belong.

BRENDA DAVIS HARSHAM

SEA HUNT

I remember the day I became a scientist.
I was seven years old.
My teacher said,
Three quarters of the earth is covered by water.
I knew it was three fifths.
Mike Nelson said so on Sea Hunt
every Saturday night.

Of course, I called her on it.
She said I was wrong,
and for the ultimate proof
she showed me where it was written
IN A BOOK.

I wasn't impressed.
I saw no reason to suppose her word
was more reliable than Mike's,
and I took it upon myself
to prove my (and Mike's) case.

My research lasted years,
and it seems the consensus
of the geophysical community
is for 70.8 percent of the earth's surface.

So technically,
both my teacher and Mike Nelson were wrong.

But the day I decided to find out for myself,
I became a scientist.

STEVEN K. SMITH

ERASE

Erase, erase, erase, erase –
However long it takes –
I've used up two erasers,
And still I spot mistakes.

A misspelled word? It has to go.
I rub 'til there's no trace.
My book report is full of holes
And looks a lot like lace.

When armed with an eraser,
I don't know when to quit.
Now my report is perfect, but
There's nothing left of it.

My book report has vanished!
I made it disappear!
A pile of dust, it floated off
Into the atmosphere,

Where everybody's bloopers merge,
And no one has to feel
Foolish or ridiculous.
Mistakes? They're no big deal.

CAROL SAMUELSON-WOODSON

PRAYER FROM THE BOTTOM OF THE BACKPACK

Backpack bristles
and bursts,
neglected homework
groans, growls,
g r o w s
angry due dates
collide.

I totter
stagger
collapse

close my eyes

pray for
snow.

BUFFY SILVERMAN

WASTING TIME

I long to run and hear the beat of my feet
  slapping the pavement
I long to read and hear the words
  jumping off the pages and humming
I long to listen to the music thumping
  until I feel like I'm flying

I know I have to concentrate but I still
Sit on the desk while the sun is sinking
And the moon has floated to the surface
The pages won't write themselves
All I have is time, the hands on the clock
Are moving so slowly, it could be under ice
My mind is completely open, it is full
Of ideas that have just crossed through

Before I know it I go into a world of fictional places
There I am able to think of anything
I can lie down without worrying
I will fall into debt to time
This moment lasts less than a minute
Soon the work is even more piled up

If I could have written down a schedule
Or made time instead of lying down
I would have been able to ace that test
I would have been able to understand each subject

But the people who wish for time waste it the most so
I long to run and here the beat of my feet
  slapping the pavement
I long to read and hear the words
  jumping off the pages and humming
I long to listen to the music thumping
  until I feel like I'm flying

REESE HOFFMAN
7TH grade

TIME BOMB

There's a time bomb

In our letterbox

Tick tick ticking

Insidiously ticking

Not one can hear it but me:

Tick tick ticking

Counting down the time

Till Mom checks the mail.

When she opens it

She will explode.

Letter from school.

SALLY MURPHY

TEMPTATION

I'm Temptation waiting to be released…
Come, sit a spell – I'm only half a beast.
I'd love your company,
We'll bond wondrously.
Kiss honesty goodbye, a sad caprice.

Climb aboard – don't think about your actions.
Mistakes are nil, only distractions.
Now, you can sneak that peek,
Mum's the word, I won't speak.
Almost there–you'll never solve that fraction.

Awww shucks, you didn't cheat; want to change your mind?
There's still some time–NO, stop, don't be so blind!
Dash-it-all, we were close,
You and I, almost pros.
Wait, I'll change my ways–Don't leave me *be-e-e-h-i-i-i-nd.*

MICHELLE KOGAN

I've never been someone
that was sort of blessed
with an innate talent
of just being able to do things.
I had to work at it
and learn from mistakes.

EDDIE REDMAYNE

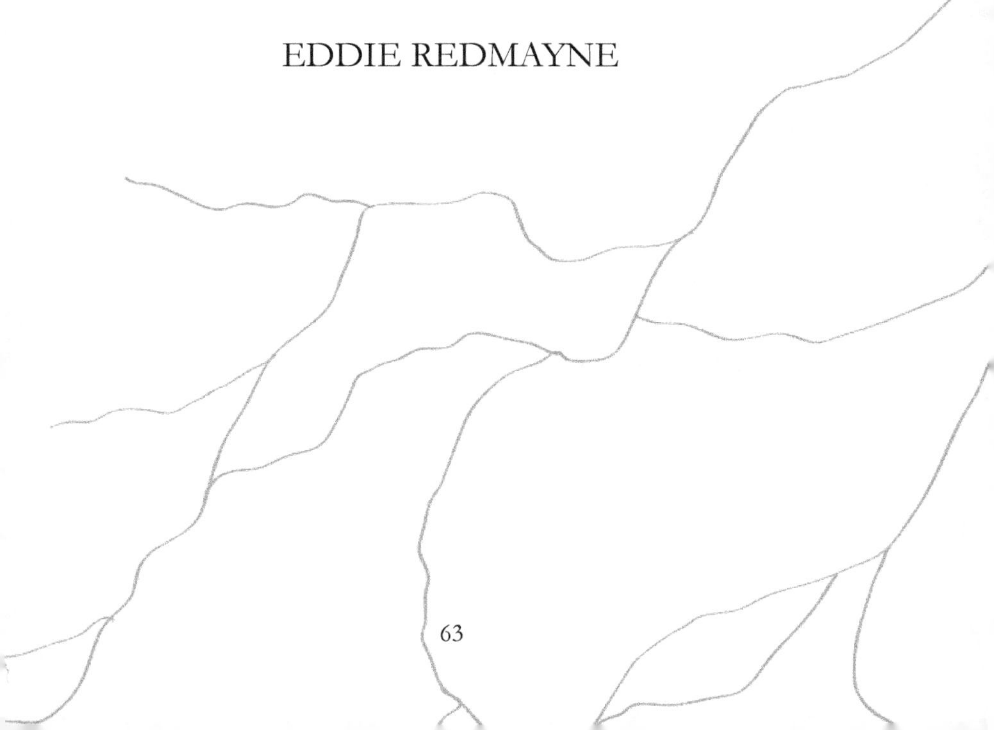

HIDDEN IN THE SEAMS

Measure.
Cut.
Pin paper pattern. Pin paper pattern.
Thread machine.
Chikita, chikita, chikita, chikita
chikita, chikita, chikita, chikita
chikita ckiki-chkkktghkCLNK

(Ugh!)
Untangle thread.
Press pieces.
Hold up.

(Argh!)
Seam ripper:
Rip rip rip rip
rip rip rip rip
Pin pin pin pin
Chikita, chikita, chikita, chikita
chikita, chikita, chikita, chikita
Zipper-time
Zippity stitchity
zip zip zip ziGGRRRP

(Ugh!)
Untangle thread.
Zippity stitchity

Zip zip zip zip
Backstitch – stitch – back – backstitch
Snip.
Press.

"You made that?"
"Yes!"

ROBYN HOOD BLACK

ORIGAMI MORNING

She slides her paper from
the colorful stack and begins:
Fold, crease, open;
Fold, crease again.

One by one, her squares transform:
crane, frog, owl, fox.

I follow her lead:
Fold, crease, open,
crease,
          slump,
                    crumple–

Smoothing out my wrinkled square,
I reach for a pencil,
breathe deeply,

find the words
that hop, hoot, howl,
          bring my paper to life.

BUFFY SILVERMAN

LAST NIGHT AS I WAS SLEEPING

(excerpt)

Last night as I was sleeping,
I dreamt—marvelous error!—
that I had a beehive
here inside my heart.
And the golden bees
were making white combs
and sweet honey
from my old failures.

ANTONIO MACHADO
translated by Robert Bly

EPIC FAIL COMPILATION

I failed my
science notebook
grade and got a
D –
Not very smart.

Nervously, I slammed my foot
against the soccer ball during
State Cup, missing
the winning penalty kick.
My teammates looked at me
and groaned so loud
you could hear it from the other
side of the field.

I was hiding in a bunker
with my friend. We were armed
with kevlar paintball-proof chest plates,
masks, and single shot
paintball guns, scanning the
terrain, when a guy with a
fully automatic paintball gun
splattered us with paintballs.
Plain dumb.

Erasing and erasing,
I shredded a huge,
2 inch hole in my
100 point essay, and
had to rewrite the
whole thing.
Just sad.

Carsick on swerving,
turning roads,
I threw up a
$40 lobster roll
in the car
on the way home from
Lake Tahoe.
Waste of money and time. Plus, it was gross.

These fails may have been
embarrassing,
stupid,
just itching to get
wiped from the memories
in my head
But I learned from every single
one of them, to not make them
again.

I shall progress
and with every step I take
I will probably make new mistakes.
But I will make sure
that those screw-ups
aren't reruns of
my past blunders.

RYAN WU
7TH grade

BACK UP

He's running faster than light
he trips he
falls and loses the
ball
everyone
laughing at him.

he c
r
i
e
s
for minutes until
he gets back up again.
He trips and falls again
wondering what he
can
do.

He DRIBBLES the ball lightning fast, side side.
to

He jumps and he DUNKS
and everyone's cheering in surprise.

ANDRES CEJA
6TH grade

DISCUS

If only
you hadn't dropped the discus on my toe
then I wouldn't have yelled at you
and you wouldn't have shouted back
then I wouldn't have called you idiot
and you wouldn't have called me a wuss
and I wouldn't have had to push you
and you wouldn't have decided to shove me back
and then our fists wouldn't have flown
and the rest of the class wouldn't have gathered around
shouting 'get him,' 'go on,' 'whoo hooo'
and then we would still
be doing sport
instead of sitting here
outside the principal's office.
If only
you hadn't dropped the discus on my toe.

SALLY MURPHY

PERFECT PAIRS

My only "F" was first grade on a workbook page
of circus pairs headed, "Circle the Likes."
I studied two ponies in equally high step,
two trapezists in exact sync. Then I saw
two clowns on stilts, though one was falling
as the other held his footing, even as
one seal balanced a ball while the other seal
was losing his balance.

I couldn't see how I could not circle them
for a mistake they'd soon recover from.
I couldn't remind them they weren't perfect pairs.
So I circled everything and failed.
But I never learned to leave the unlikes.
Even now when bowed seals and fallen clowns
call to me in my dreams, I say to them,
"Sure, come on in. You can be in my show!"

DIANE KENDIG

BITTER CHOCOLATE

I remember an early Easter morning
at my grandparents' house in Florida.
My sister whispered to me,
"Go look for your basket."
I was uncertain, hesitant.
"Go on," she urged.
So I did.
Not pausing to wonder why she didn't.
Blinded by my sweet tooth,
eager to see that grass-filled basket
filled with a tumble of toys and treats,
I searched until
Eureka!
I found it!
My laden basket
hidden behind a heavy curtain.
I knelt and my small hand reached out,
grabbed and unwrapped
a miniature chocolate bunny,
popped it into my grinning mouth.
Chocolate for breakfast!
Treasure in hand, I turned
to see two dark polished shoes
planted in the plush carpet,
long creased pant legs attached.
Slowly I rose
basket dangling in my hand.
I looked up, up, up to see
my grandfather's face,
stern and frowning,
disappointment writ large.
"What are you doing?"
he rumbled.

"You're not supposed to look for your basket yet!"
In an instant
my delight melted
as completely
as the chocolate in my mouth.
It left a
lingering,
bitter
taste.

MOLLY HOGAN

SCARED OF COWS

I wasn't always
scared of cows,
my mum says.
As a 3 year-old
I used to herd them
into the bails
for milking,
and even the bull
didn't worry me,
my mum says.

'Never come
between a cow
and her calf,'
my dad said,
squatting down
to comfort
5 year-old me
as I quivered
and cried.
And never forgot.

KAT APEL

The web of our life is of a mingled yarn,
good and ill together.

WILLIAM SHAKESPEARE

THREE-ALARM MISTAKES

involve hospitals

like the time my stepbrother dared me to climb to the swing-set top, and I learned gravity hurts

or the time the drunk driver swerved in the rain, and our Volkswagen Bug couldn't fly, despite its name.

The kind that breaks and remakes your life. The kind you don't forget, not ever.

So different from two-alarm mistakes that leave no scars (No hospitals!)

but still transform your life

like the time I laughed with the whole class at the pimply boy who tripped over his backpack, only to see him crying behind his hand (The look on his face is the one in the bathroom mirror when my father disses me.)

or the time the blind student rocked in her chair, the other kids laughed and I realized that no one had sat within two rows of her for weeks. (I remembered the pimply boy. I be-friended her, despite knowing they'd be laughing at me next.)

Then the one-alarm mistakes,
the ones where I stain my shirt,
or smile with spinach in my teeth all day,
or forget to take the trash barrels to the curb

the ladders I climb,

each step teaches me to
lean forward when I eat,
check the mirror after lunch and
leave myself post-its on the wall.

I inch-worm my way, tiny alarms jangling, hoping to take
embarrassing moments in stride

like my grandmother does when
she naps, drools, at the dinner table,
wakes up, mops her face with a napkin and says,
"The sandman's out of sand. I'm calling him riverman."

And I'm happy every day
I don't have an
elbow-cast on a pillow,
(throb, THROB, throb, THROB)
while the green digital clock
illuminates the nurse's heart
drawn on my cast and the numbers
buzz from four-digit time to three.

BRENDA DAVIS HARSHAM

STOLEN

It wasn't mine.
It isn't.
I didn't mean to steal it.
It was so soft
and small enough
to fit in the palm
of my hand.
I hid it
in my pocket,
but now I wish
I hadn't.
What used to be
my secret prize
feels like a hole
in my stomach.

ELIZABETH STEINGLASS

TO THE BOY PLAYING WITH HIS ARMY MEN ON THE FRONT LAWN:

They say that everyone is fighting some kind of battle,
but I have no good excuse for my surprise attack—
a ride-by on bicycle, words flung like a grenade.
I wanted to hear the pop of the pin,
taste the insult in my mouth,
feel my heart pound in the moments before the blast.
And then it was done.
(I couldn't take it back.)
I pedal away feeling like the enemy—
even to myself.

MICHELLE HEIDENRICH BARNES

PEELING YOUR WORDS AWAY

Are you sorry?

I don't know,
but I have your
wounding words

splashed across
my brain and heart
like spray-painted letters –

careless,
neon,
and eye-catching –

how can I think other thoughts
with these here,
taking up all the room?

I carefully
peel up the words
like stickers,

letter by letter,
tugging at the edges
and pulling carefully –

when they rip,
I start over,
picking from another side

until finally...
they all come loose,
flimsy and flat,

so I crumple them up
and toss them away.

TABATHA YEATTS

SO TALL

Puny kid, please tell me why,
why as the week went rolling by,
by and by, you stood so tall.

I bullied you. I did it all.

Puny kid, you know it's true,
true, I shouldn't have bullied you.
You forgave me in the end.

My mistake, my giant friend.

KEN SLESARIK

LOTS OF THINGS

I've got lots of things to tell you.
When I passed you in the hall,
there were just too many things to say,
so I said none at all.

I've got lots of things to tell you.
Why'd I look the other way?
Why'd I hurry off in such a rush
and barely blurt out, "Hey"?

I've got lots of things to tell you.
Yeah, I blew it. Yeah, it stings.
I swear if there's a second chance,
I'll tell you lots of things.

SUZY LEVINSON

THE WORD

(excerpt)

Oh, a word is a gem, or a stone, or a song,
Or a flame, or a two-edged sword;
Or a rose in bloom, or a sweet perfume,
Or a drop of gall is a word.

You may choose your word like a connoisseur,
And polish it up with art,
But the word that sways, and stirs, and stays,
Is the word that comes from the heart.

ELLA WHEELER WILCOX

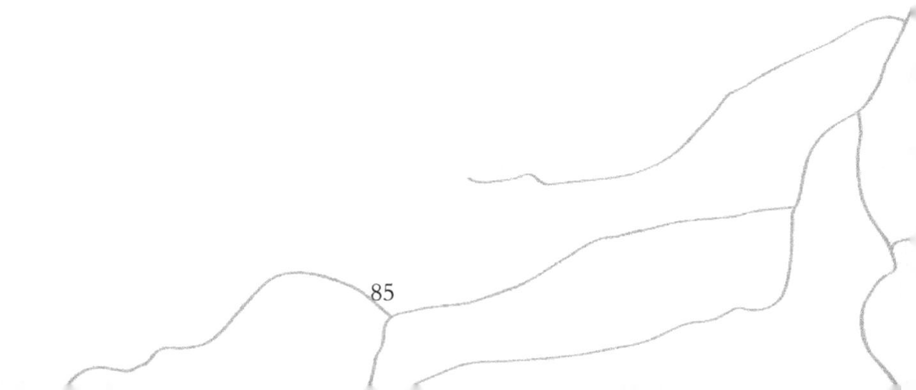

Life is a succession of lessons
which must be lived to be understood.

RALPH WALDO EMERSON

EVERYDAY WRONGDOINGS

Mom taps her foot.
Arms crossed
She looks down at me,
The way only she can.
Making me feel *that* way,
Like only she can make me feel.

This was not a major transgression.
Not like the time:
I broke my sister's finger
Or,
I let the dog out and he ran away
Or,
I dropped an entire pot of soup on the kitchen floor as I was helping Dad
Or…

Those became stories,
Unfolded like napkins at the dinner table,
Thanksgiving,
4th of July.
Whenever there was a crowd who would laugh,
Even if I wasn't laughing, too.

This was different.
Normal.
Everyday wrongdoings.

Nothing broken but a tiny piece of my heart
Nothing lost except some momentary measure of trust.

Nothing spilt except some tears,
As I watch Mom
Watch me
With that look,
Looking down.

"You still love me, right?"

BETH BRODY

MY GRANDFATHER'S HAND

My grandfather's hand had no thumb,
no stump, dug out at the joint,
its absence leaving a strange shape
from his forefinger to his wrist.
From the cellar steps I watched him
build a perpetual motion machine,
carpenter toys—my doll bed
was lacquered jet red by that hand
I never minded at work. But I hated
it whenever he leaned to kiss me.
Now he is gone, but I see his difference
differently, remember how
nobody else ever held my face so gently.

DIANE KENDIG

THE LAWS OF MOTION

The first time I saw you,
your face reminded me of the scarred,
pock-marked surface of Io,
Jupiter's volcanic moon.

How brave you were to walk
into that unknown space,
carrying a plastic tray filled
with tater tots,
as if that would shield you
from the shining stars
of our little galaxy.

A comet sailed among us that year,
pulled me into his orbit,
blinded me to right and wrong,
caused me to wobble on my axis
until I was so off-kilter that
I didn't say a word
when he turned to you,
pelted you with cruelty and insults.

To this day, I'm ashamed
I wasn't strong enough
to pull free of his hold on me.
Ashamed that I didn't have your strength,

that I looked away,
as you strode by
with your head held high.

CATHERINE FLYNN

DO-OVER

When I got paired with the new girl,
I rolled my eyes and groaned.

I was happy when she whispered,
I'll just work alone.

But now I can't stop thinking,
about the sadness in her voice.

If I could do it over,
kindness would be my choice.

LINDA KULP TROUT

WORDS

I made a mistake, I'm sorry to say.
I made a mistake in speaking today.

I thought it was funny but you didn't see,
So now my great joke's been thrown back at me.

I hurt your feelings - I can't take words back;
Those words that I said seemed like an attack.

I thought that you'd laugh - I didn't mean it;
But you looked away, I should have seen it.

I struck a bare nerve, exceedingly raw;
I should have known better, but too late I saw

That I'd cut to the core where it's slow to heal;
I should have known how my words would feel.

And now I just wait hoping you can forgive me,
But I wouldn't blame you if your anger outlived me.

I'm sorry, so sorry! Is this where it ends?
What's that you said? We still can be friends?

Apology accepted? (Huge sigh of relief)
I promise forever to give you no grief!

Friends don't hurt friends with words or in works
Friends are forever - so I'll work on my quirks!

DONNA JT SMITH

STUPIDITY

Dearest, forgive that with my clumsy touch
I broke and bruised your rose.
I hardly could suppose
It were a thing so fragile that my clutch
Could kill it, thus.

It stood so proudly up upon its stem,
I knew no thought of fear,
And coming very near
Fell, overbalanced, to your garment's hem,
Tearing it down.

Now, stooping, I upgather, one by one,
The crimson petals, all
Outspread about my fall.
They hold their fragrance still, a blood-red cone
Of memory.

And with my words I carve a little jar
To keep their scented dust,
Which, opening, you must
Breathe to your soul, and, breathing, know me far
More grieved than you.

AMY LOWELL

Was it you or I who stumbled first?
It does not matter.
The one of us who finds the strength
to get up first, must help the other.

VERA NAZARIAN

THE JUNK BOX

My father often used to say:
"My boy don't throw a thing away:
You'll find a use for it some day."

So in a box he stored up things,
Bent nails, old washers, pipes and rings,
And bolts and nuts and rusty springs.

Despite each blemish and each flaw,
Some use for everything he saw;
With things material, this was law.

And often when he'd work to do,
He searched the junk box through and through
And found old stuff as good as new.

And I have often thought since then,
That father did the same with men;
He knew he'd need their help again.

It seems to me he understood
That men, as well as iron and wood,
May broken be and still be good.

Despite the vices he'd display
He never threw a man away,
But kept him for another day.

A human junk box is this earth
And into it we're tossed at birth,
To wait the day we'll be of worth.

Though bent and twisted, weak of will,
And full of flaws and lacking skill,
Some service each can render still.

EDGAR ALBERT GUEST

TO KNOW ALL IS TO FORGIVE ALL

IF I KNEW YOU and you knew me —
If both of us could clearly see,
And with an inner sight divine
The meaning of your heart and mine —
I'm sure that we would differ less
And clasp our hands in friendliness;
Our thoughts would pleasantly agree
If I knew you, and you knew me.

If I knew you and you knew me,
As each one knows his own self, we
Could look each other in the face
And see therein a truer grace.
Life has so many hidden woes,
So many thorns for every rose;
The "why" of things our hearts would see,
If I knew you and you knew me.

NIXON WATERMAN

OUTWITTED

He drew a circle that shut me out –
Heretic, a rebel, a thing to flout.
But Love and I had the wit to win:
We drew a circle that took him in!

EDWIN MARKHAM

MAGIC FORMULA TO MAKE AN ENEMY PEACEFUL

Pollen is the Navajo emblem of peace and this is the equivalent to saying: Put your feet down in peace, and so on.

Put your feet down with pollen.
Put your hands down with pollen.
Put your head down with pollen.
Then your feet are pollen;
Your hands are pollen;
Your body is pollen;
Your mind is pollen;
Your voice is pollen.
The trail is beautiful.
Be still.

A NAVAJO POEM
translated by Washington Matthews

FORGIVENESS

closed door
between me and you
knocking

MICHELLE HEIDENRICH BARNES

NEW EVERY MORNING

(excerpt)

All the past things are past and over;
The tasks are done and the tears are shed.
Yesterday's errors let yesterday cover;
Yesterday's wounds, which smarted and bled,
Are healed with the healing which night has shed.

SUSAN COOLIDGE

Out of difficulties grow miracles.

JEAN DE LA BRUYERE

MAKING GOOD DECISIONS: BRAINSTORMING FOR FUTURE YOU

One of the reasons we make mistakes every day is that we have to make decisions every day. How can we make it more likely that we're making good ones?

* Gather information. What choices do you have? What are their pros and cons? Are you sure you've thought of all the possibilities? Your first idea might not be your BEST idea... brainstorming is smart!

* Consider your options. Have you ever heard of something being "first-order positive, second-order negative"? What does that mean?

That means that the first thing that happens is enjoyable, but the follow-up isn't. For instance, you stay up late watching a movie instead of studying for the exam you have early the next morning. Staying up was fun, but being tired, not thinking clearly, and not knowing the answers during the exam isn't.

People who make choices that are the opposite – first-order negative, second-order positive – have an advantage. They do the less fun stuff first, but good stuff happens later. For instance, those are the folks who save money to buy something special or train hard and then make the team.

The way you can think about it is, "How will Future Me feel about this decision I'm making?" If Future You will say thanks, that's a sign that you are making a good decision.

If you want to ask someone their advice about what you should do, take a second to think "Does this person have my best interests in mind?" Sometimes people's advice will be affected by their own interests, which may not match your own. For instance, a classmate might encourage you to do something that they would find entertaining to watch, but would get you in trouble. Or someone might encourage you not to try out for something because they don't want the competition. If you are asking for advice, seek it from people who are looking out for YOU.

* After you've made your decision and taken action, don't forget to review how your choice went. Here's your chance to learn something and get ideas for next time!

APOLOGIZING EFFECTIVELY

Have you ever been told "Sorry" in a way that sounds like the person wasn't the tiniest bit sorry? Some apologies are more annoying than comforting. When you've made a mistake and want to apologize, how can you express it so you have the best shot of actually making the other person feel better?

* For starters, sound like you mean it. Don't just say, "sorry," say, "I'm really sorry." If you wish you hadn't done it, say so.

* Be sure to reassure them that you won't do it again. Apologizing and then doing it again comes off like you weren't really sorry the first time.

* Listen to what the other person has to say. Everyone likes to be heard. They might want to make sure you know how they feel or tell you what you need to do to make it up to them.

* What if the other person also did something wrong? Say specifically what you are sorry for, the actions you wish you hadn't done. If you take responsibility for your mistakes, you will feel good about yourself, even if you don't wind up feeling better about the other person's actions. That's on them.

* It can be hard to move past a mistake without apologizing, so even when saying you're sorry is tough, give it your best shot.

POEM FORMS YOU CAN TRY

ACROSTIC

With an acrostic, the first letter (or first word) of each line spells something when you read it horizontally. An example is **Mistakes-sekatsiM** by Donna JT Smith.

DIAMANTE

Diamantes are diamond-shaped poems that follow this pattern:

Noun
Adjective, Adjective
Verb, Verb, Verb
Noun, Noun, Noun, Noun
Verb, Verb, Verb
Adjective, Adjective
Noun

You can begin and end with synonyms or antonyms. Linda Mitchell used antonyms with her poem **Mistake.**

DOUBLE DACTYL

Double dactyls are challenging light verse poems. They have a lot of rules. In fact, it's easier to understand double dactyls by looking at examples, like Christy Mihaly's poems **The Alaska Purchase** and **Rejecting Harry Potter**.

Double dactyls have eight lines of two dactyls each, arranged in two stanzas. The first line of the poem must be a nonsense phrase; the second line must be a name; and the last lines of each stanza should rhyme. A line in the second stanza must be only one word of six syllables. Some people say that you should use a six-syllable word that has never been used in a double dactyl before!

POEMS FOR TWO VOICES

A poem for two voices is a dialogue between two people (or two of something else) that gives two different points of view and is meant to be performed. It usually has three columns – one on the left and right for each of the points-of-view, plus one in the middle when they speak together. You can see an example with **Mistaken Identity: a poem for two voices** by Keri Collins Lewis.

ACKNOWLEDGMENTS

My Grandfather's Hand by Diane Kendig appeared in *The Louisville Review.*
Anaconda Surprise by Irene Latham appeared in *Action Magazine* (Scholastic, Inc.).
Titanic Remembers April 16, 1912 by Irene Latham appeared in *Storyworks Magazine* (Scholastic, Inc.).
In the Archive by Patrick Williams appeared in *Nine Mile Magazine.*

The Leaning Tower of Pisa appears courtesy photographer Saffron Blaze, Creative Commons licensing.
Cherry Blossoms @ Burrard Station (Sakura) appears courtesy photographer GoToVan, Creative Commons licensing.
RMS Titanic is by F.G.O. Stuart and is in the public domain.
A Little Girl Making Bowties appears courtesy photographer Zing Shotz, Creative Commons licensing.
Honeycomb appears courtesy photographer Monika Fischer, Creative Commons licensing.
Fierce Cow appears courtesy photographer Kat Apel.

The Team Imperfect blog is located at
https://mistakesanthology.blogspot.com/

Please join us!

CPSIA information can be obtained
at www.ICGtesting.com
Printed in the USA
LVHW042307290519
619456LV00013BA/674/P